I0816451

AROUND TOWN

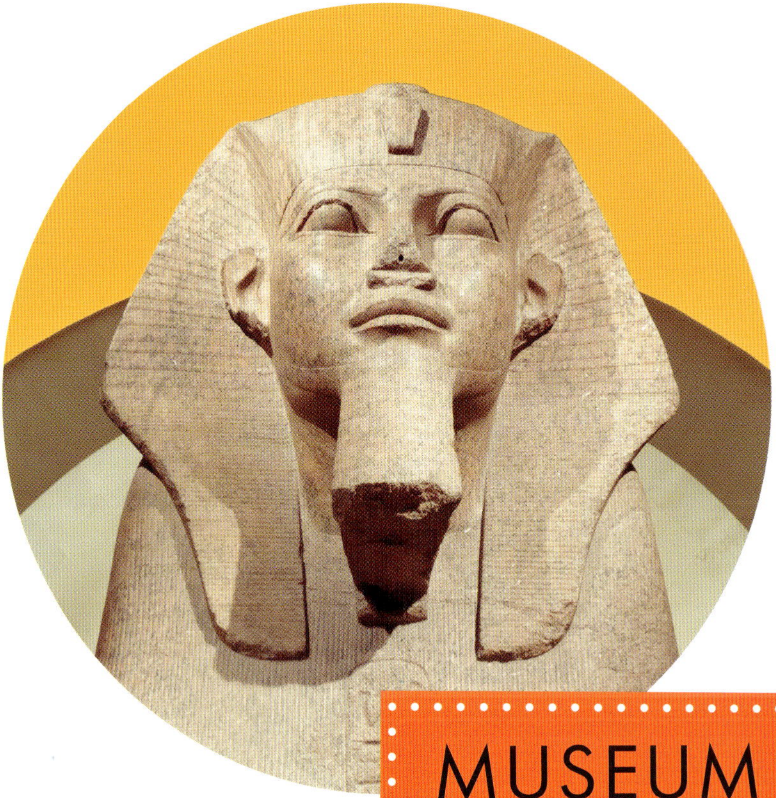

MUSEUM

by Alissa Thielges

lobby

screen

Look for these words and pictures as you read.

painting

fossils

Let's go to the museum!
What will we see?

Museums teach about the past. They have art and science.

Look at the lobby.
This is where you enter.
You can buy a ticket.

lobby

Priser
Prices
Priser på klubkort
Klub Moesgaard
Den Første Kejser
Kinas terrakottahær
SÆRUDSTILLING

painting

Look at the painting.
A famous artist made it.
It is beautiful!

fossils

Look at the fossils.
They are very old bones.
They come from a dinosaur!

Look at the screen.
Owen touches it.
He learns about bugs.

screen

The gift shop is by the exit.
Kai buys a book.
What a great trip!

lobby

screen

Did you find?

painting

fossils

Spot is published by Amicus and Amicus Ink
P.O. Box 227, Mankato, MN 56002
www.amicuspublishing.us

Library of Congress Cataloging-in-Publication Data
Names: Thielges, Alissa, 1995– author.
Title: Museum / by Alissa Thielges.
Description: Mankato, MN : Amicus Learning, [2025] | Series: Spot around town | Audience: Ages 4–7 | Audience: Grades K–1 | Summary: "A search-and-find book about museums reinforces new vocabulary to build reading success while close-up images of places and buildings captivate young audiences. A great early social studies book to inspire learning about communities on field trips for kindergartners and first graders"– Provided by publisher.
Identifiers: LCCN 2023045010 (print) | LCCN 2023045011 (ebook) | ISBN 9781645497356 (hardcover) | ISBN 9781645497431 (ebook)
Subjects: LCSH: Museums–Juvenile literature.
Classification: LCC AM5 .T55 2025 (print) | LCC AM5 (ebook) | DDC 069–dc23/eng/20230925
LC record available at https://lccn.loc.gov/2023045010
LC ebook record available at https://lccn.loc.gov/2023045011

Printed in China

Rebecca Glaser, editor
Deb Miner, series designer
Kim Pfeffer, book designer and photo researcher

Photos by Alamy Stock Photo/Hufton+Crow-VIEW, 6–7; Kumar Sriskandan, 14; Dreamstime/Agaliza, 1; Lisa Mckown, 3; Shutterstock/Anton_Ivanov, 8–9; Evikka, 12–13; Puwadol Jaturawutthichai, 10–11; Trong Nguyen, cover; The Noun Project/Carol M. Highsmith, 4–5